How Orcus Stole Christmas!

Author	5E Conversion	Art Direction
James M. Spahn	Scott Mckinley & Edwin Nagy	Casey W. Christofferson
Producer	**Fantasy Grounds Conversion**	**Front Cover Art**
Bill Webb	Michael G. Potter	Terry Pavlet
Project Manager	**Layout and Graphic Design**	**Interior Art**
Zach Glazar	Charles A. Wright	Joshua Stewart, Casey W. Christofferson
Editor	**Cover Design**	**Cartography**
Jeff Harkness	Jim Wampler	Robert Altbauer

FROG GOD GAMES IS

CEO	Production Director	Special Projects Director
Bill Webb	Charles A. Wright	Jim Wampler
Creative Director	**Chief of Operations**	**Customer Relations**
Matthew J. Finch	Zach Glazar	Mike Badalato

FROG GOD GAMES

5TH EDITION RULES, 1ST EDITION FEEL

Other Products from Frog God Games

You can find these product lines and more at our website, **froggodgames.com**, and on the shelves of many retail game stores. Superscripts indicate the available game systems: "PF" means the Pathfinder Roleplaying Game, "5e" means Fifth Edition, and "S&W" means *Swords & Wizardry*. If there is no superscript it means that it is not specific to a single rule system.

GENERAL RESOURCES

Swords & Wizardry Complete [S&W]
Tome of Horrors [5E]
The Tome of Horrors Complete [PF, S&W]
Tome of Horrors 4 [PF, S&W]
Tome of Adventure Design
Monstrosities [S&W]
Bill Webb's Book of Dirty Tricks
Razor Coast: Fire as She Bears [PF]
Book of Lost Spells [5e, PF]
Fifth Edition Foes [5e]
The Tome of Blighted Horrors [5e, PF, S&W]

THE LOST LANDS

Rappan Athuk [PF, S&W, 5E]
Rappan Athuk Expansions Vol. I [PF, S&W]
The Slumbering Tsar Saga [PF]
The Black Monastery [PF, S&W]
Cyclopean Deeps Vol. I [PF, S&W]
Cyclopean Deeps Vol. II [PF, S&W]
Razor Coast [PF, S&W]
Razor Coast: Heart of the Razor [PF, S&W]
Razor Coast: Freebooter's Guide to the Razor Coast [PF, S&W]
LL0: The Lost Lands Campaign Setting* [5e, PF, S&W]
LL1: Stoneheart Valley [PF, S&W]

LL2: The Lost City of Barakus [PF, S&W]
LL3: Sword of Air [PF, S&W]
LL4: Cults of the Sundered Kingdoms [PF, S&W]
LL5: Borderland Provinces [5e, PF, S&W]
LL6: The Northlands Saga Complete [PF, S&W]
LL7: The Blight [5e, PF, S&W]
LL8: Bard's Gate [5e, PF, S&W]
LL9: Adventures in the Borderland Provinces [5e, PF, S&W]

QUESTS OF DOOM

Quests of Doom (Vol. 1) [5e]
Quests of Doom (Vol. 2) [5e]
Quests of Doom (includes the 5e Vol. 1 and 2, but for PF and S&W only) [PF, S&W]
Quests of Doom 2 [5e]
Quests of Doom 3 [5e, S&W]
Quests of Doom 4 [5e, PF, S&W]

PERILOUS VISTAS

Dead Man's Chest (pdf only) [PF]
Dunes of Desolation [PF]
Fields of Blood [PF]
Mountains of Madness [PF]
Marshes of Malice [PF]

* (forthcoming from **Frog God Games**)

Table of Contents

How Orcus Stole Christmas!

By James M. Spahn

How Orcus Stole Christmas! is a short adventure for 4–6 characters between levels 3–5. After being hired by a local baron to deliver much-needed supplies to a rural village, the characters discover that a tribe of strange creatures led by the cheerfully violent Orcus' Claws has ransacked the town and set up a workshop crafting toys that promise only death and destruction instead of holiday cheer.

Adventure Background

No one knows where the demonic thing calling himself Orcus' Claws came from, only that he has with him a tribe of goblinoids known as the Crueltide elves. Claws came into town wearing a mantle that may once have been white, but was now stained a cheerfully blood red. The Crueltide elves, under the command of their dark master, ransacked the village of Newville and took every conceivable piece of technology the villagers had. They stole hammers, anvils, nails, hinges, iron tools, entire doors, and even the wheels from the carts of local merchants.

With no resources to protect themselves from the winter snowstorms, the villagers of Newville turn to the characters for aid, claiming that Orcus' Claws and his Crueltide elves fled into the snow-covered pine forest to the north. Since that fateful night, they have seen plumes of smoke rising on the horizon. Claws and his Elves are crafting some terrible holiday surprise, and without the aid of the characters, the people of Newville will be left only with holiday fear instead of holiday cheer.

Beginning the Adventure

This adventure can easily be introduced into any cold-weather rural area. The characters either come upon the village of Newville in their travels or are tasked by a local noble to travel to the village to make sure they are well supplied for the winter. Another possibility is that human or halfling characters have particularly eccentric cousins who live in Newville, and the characters have been invited to the annual Winter Festival celebration.

If the characters are acting in the employ of a local noble, they are offered a reward of 100 gp each by that local lord once they return with news that the villagers of Newville are in good health for the winter.

Regardless of the party's reasons for traveling to Newville, you can read or paraphrase the text below to begin the adventure.

> You and your companions come over the rolling hill to see the forested valley under the shadow of Mount Strumpet. A large clearing where the village of Newville sits is surrounded by endless banks of twinkling white snow in the light of the winter dawn. The icy tranquility of what would otherwise be a breathtaking view is marred by thin tendrils of smoke rising from various cottages and buildings that are visible even from this distance.
>
> As you and your companions quicken your pace down the last ridge and into the valley of the village proper, you see that destruction has been visited upon this idyllic rural community. Several corpses lie in bloodstained snowbanks, and the wails of villagers wracked with pain and sorrow break even the snow-muffled silence of winter. Something far worse than a bad fruitcake has been visited upon this winter wonderland...

Part One:

What's New Down in Newville

The village of Newville is home to no more than 500 residents who make their living hunting local game in order to trade meat and fur, or through harvesting local lumber. Many of the villagers are halflings, and all seem somehow related, collectively calling themselves the News of Newville (a custom happily adopted by everyone who moves into the burgeoning village). A diminutive and cherubic halfling woman with blonde hair named Lucinda New leads the villagers of Newville. Her annoyingly positive demeanor reflects the general sense of almost idiotic happiness that typically fills the village.

Unfortunately, all that changed last night during the fifth night of the Newville Winter Festival. Orcus' Claws and his Crueltide elves swept into the village while every single person in the village was gathered around the Festival Tree in the center of town. Silently and stealthily, these nefarious creatures stole every piece of metal and every tool they could get their hands on. From tiny screws pried from window frames to massive iron cellar doors, the Crueltide elves stole it all. Then, at the stroke of midnight, after Claws and his Elves hauled the stolen loot to their secret lair atop Mount Strumpet, they came charging into the village and began to slaughter the News living in Newville. After several formerly musical News were left dead and the village was in shambles, Claws and his Crueltide elves fled into the night with cries that they would return for "Twelve Bloody Nights of Clawsmas."

The characters arrive in Newville the morning after the first attack. Most of the villagers are sullenly attempting to recover from the attack, gathering their dead, propping up crude wooden doors to lean into their frames, or building primitive lean-tos to get some meager protection from the once-beloved winter landscape.

Halfling Mayor Lucinda New, along with the human sheriff Vern Wourelle, ask for the characters' aid in recovering their stolen metal and beseech them to prevent Orcus' Claws and his Crueltide Elves from returning.

1-1: Eastern Fields

A thick blanket of snow pockmarked by blood and dirt covers this long, low valley. As you and your companions make your way toward the village, you see several small huts that were undoubtedly homes to the farmers who tend these fields in the warm season. Most now lie in ruin. Collapsed houses and crumbled stables are all that remain of most of these simple and welcoming homes. Several humans and halflings are sullenly dragging the corpses of their fellow villagers from the snow or futilely attempting to repair their broken homes.

The locals (**commoners** with 80% chance of being halflings) are a strange lot, as often singing quietly to themselves as they are weeping. They have little to say to the characters, save for a few mentions of Orcus' Claws and his terrible Crueltide elves. If asked for more detail, villagers simply begin to cry pathetically and ask to be left to their sorrows.

Those not digging graves and tending to the slain stand near their collapsed homes, muttering to themselves about how they're going to be able to repair the damage done to their collapsed homes. Several of these would-be repairmen are holding tools that have had their metal parts removed: hammers without heads, saws without blades, and the like. If asked what happened to their tools, a few mutter about the Crueltide elves (whom they describe as tooth-mawed creatures with beady red eyes and strangely pointed ears and shoes), while others say they do not want to speak of it and that the characters are better off speaking to Lucinda New, the mayor of Newville.

1-2: Lumber Yard

The fields just north of Newville are filled with downed trees from the nearby forest. It is strangely quiet, with a blanket of snow hangs over the entire scene. Long, heavy logs sit in silent tribute to the industriousness of the sturdy News, though a great pile of felled timbers is buried beneath the roof of a now collapsed open-walled covering that recently came crashing down. Several dwarves and humans are milling about, each impossibly attempting to dig the valuable lumber free from this mountain of collapsed wood, all the while screaming frantically to one another.

As the characters approach, a dwarf yells for them to help. Bernard (lawful good male dwarf **commoner** with Strength 16 and +4 on Intelligence checks concerning lumber or woodwork) tells the characters that several lumberyard workers are trapped under the rubble. Sadly, all the pulleys, flywheels, winch cables, and other pieces of technology were stolen, and they're unable to lift the rubble. As the characters draw close to the rubble, they hear the hoarse cries of several workers (**commoners** with 80% chance of being halflings) trapped in the rubble.

Getting them free is no easy task with no perfect way to solve the problem. Working with the others to pull rubble away is a long and backbreaking process, taking hours and is not likely to save the buried workers. By making creative use of their own resources, the large beams of wood, and even any spells they might have, the characters may be able to assist in the rescue effort. Using large timbers to create levers, casting spells such as *levitate*, and other clever methods will certainly be the order of the day. If the characters are clever and resourceful, reward out-of-the-box thinking with at least some likelihood of success.

A total of four workers are buried in the rubble. For every 15 minutes that pass without a successful rescue, one of the buried workers dies. This means that all will be dead within an hour.

Regardless of whether the characters are successful, Bernard thanks them for their help. In the event they rescue one or more of the workers, Bernard is exceedingly thankful. Though he has no money to offer them, he instead gives them a flask of his special dwarven fire spirits liquor. The flasks contain four drams of *frozen concoction*[2].

1-3: Festival Tree

A massive pine tree covered in candles of bright wax, wrapped in strings of nuts, candied fruits, and lovingly polished apples sits in the center of the tiny village of Newville. It is a forty-foot testament to unwavering holiday cheer crowned with a twinkling silver star. Several News mill about the tree, halfheartedly singing cheerful songs that sound all the more mournful for their attempts.

Among the crowd of a dozen or so, one New stands out: a halfling woman with an exceedingly round face, wild golden curls, and eyes as bright and shining as the winter sky. She trundles up to you and your companions, wiping the tears from her eyes and taking a moment to obviously compose herself before putting on a bright and innocent smile. "Lucinda New, Mayor of Newville! Welcome to our village — and merry Wintermass!"

Despite her attempts at holiday cheer, she appears on the verge of bursting into tears as she holds out a sausage-fingered hand in greeting.

Lucinda New (lawful good female halfling **commoner** with Dexterity 14 and Wisdom 15) is genuinely polite with the characters and apologizes to them, as what is normally a cheerful time for the Village of Newville has turned to tragedy. In a whisper, she says she doesn't want to speak about the details of what happened so as not to remind the townsfolk of the tragedy, but if the characters would like to come to her house, she'll gladly explain the situation to them over dinner.

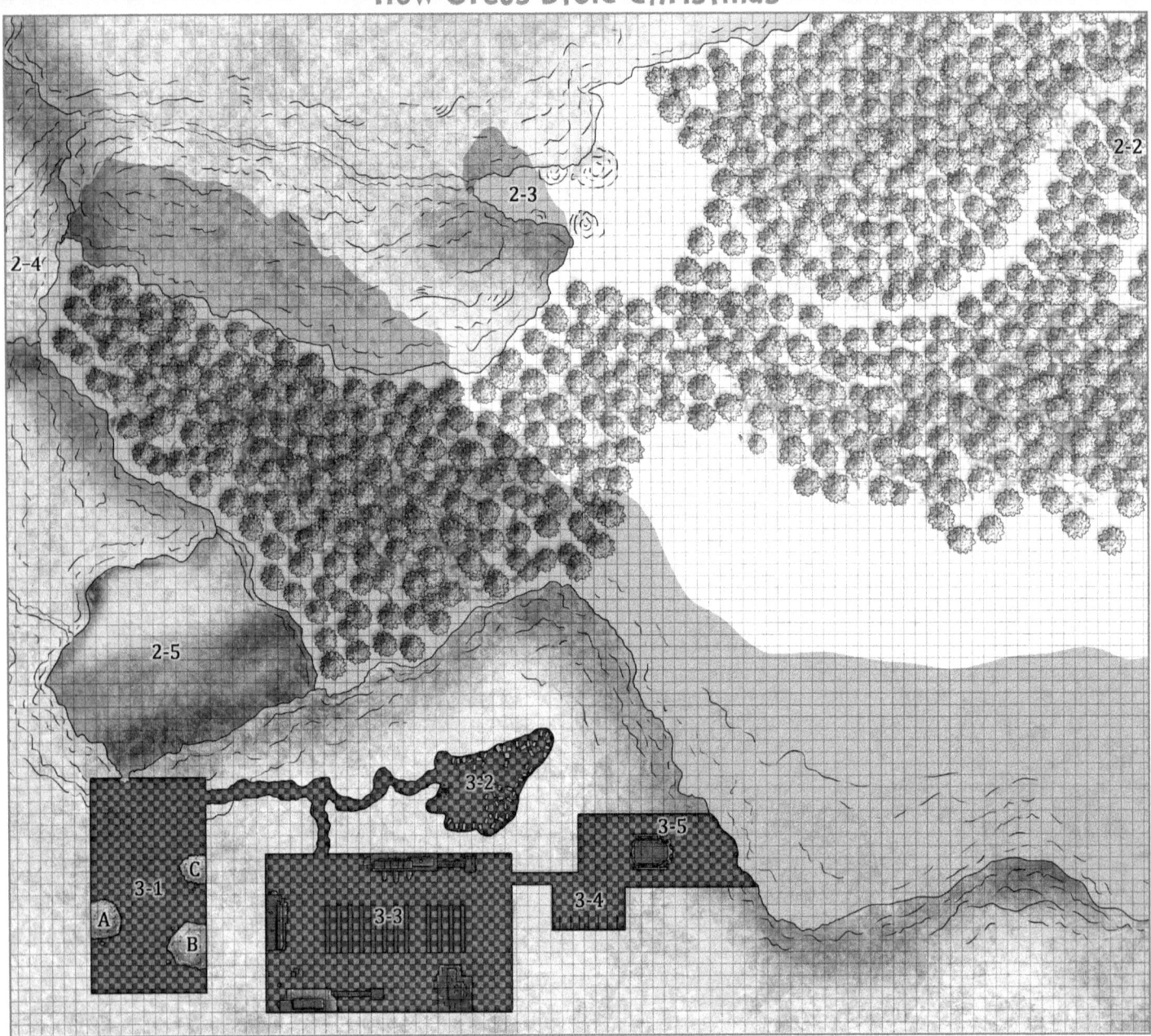

While Lucinda and the characters are talking, a small halfling boy on tiny crutches approaches, holding out one hand covered in a frayed glove. He demurely asks the characters if they can spare a copper coin or two, what with it being Winter Festival and all. He then coughs pathetically. If given a coin, he tips his ragged cap to them and hobbles away with a weak smile on his face.

Lucinda explains that the boy is "Small Sam" (lawful good male halfling **commoner** with Strength 6, Constitution 6, and a Speed of 15 ft.). Without shelter or resources and given the current developments in Newville, the boy likely will die of his crippling illness. Lucinda turns away and tells the characters to come by her home around sunset. Those who look closely see that she is crying, though she tries to hide it as she walks away.

The Festival Tree itself is a massive natural pine tree brightly decorated in celebration of the season. While characters are more than welcome to admire it, those attempting to touch it are given discouraging looks by the locals unless they show signs of trying to assist in righting a few of the misplaced decorations. If they blatantly attempt to harm or dismantle the tree, the Newville locals (**commoners** with 80% chance of being halflings) order them to stop and may even attack the characters if they don't desist.

1-4: Lucinda New's House

This simple one-room cottage is a bit larger than the others in Newville, though its door lies in a nearby snowbank. Wisps of white snow blow across the threshold and into the house itself. Inside, a large empty spot below a hole in the ceiling is where a cooking stove undoubtedly once stood. The timbers of a bed frame lie in the opposite corner. All the furniture in the room appears to have been disassembled down to its base parts. Even the nails that once held up the family portraits are gone.

If the characters arrive here near dusk, they find that Lucinda has set up a crude fire pit of dirt in a ring of stone *inside* her home. She's gathered some wet twigs into a pile and is attempting to light them with a flint. Unfortunately, she is not succeeding. If the characters were invited, Lucinda welcomes them into her home with an apology that she has no hot tea nor a warm dinner to offer them. All she has is cold pork, half a wheel of cheese, and part of a loaf of crusty bread. If they were not invited, she invites them in and says she welcomes guests, even in these dark times.

Over the cold meal and empty fire pit, Lucinda explains that last night

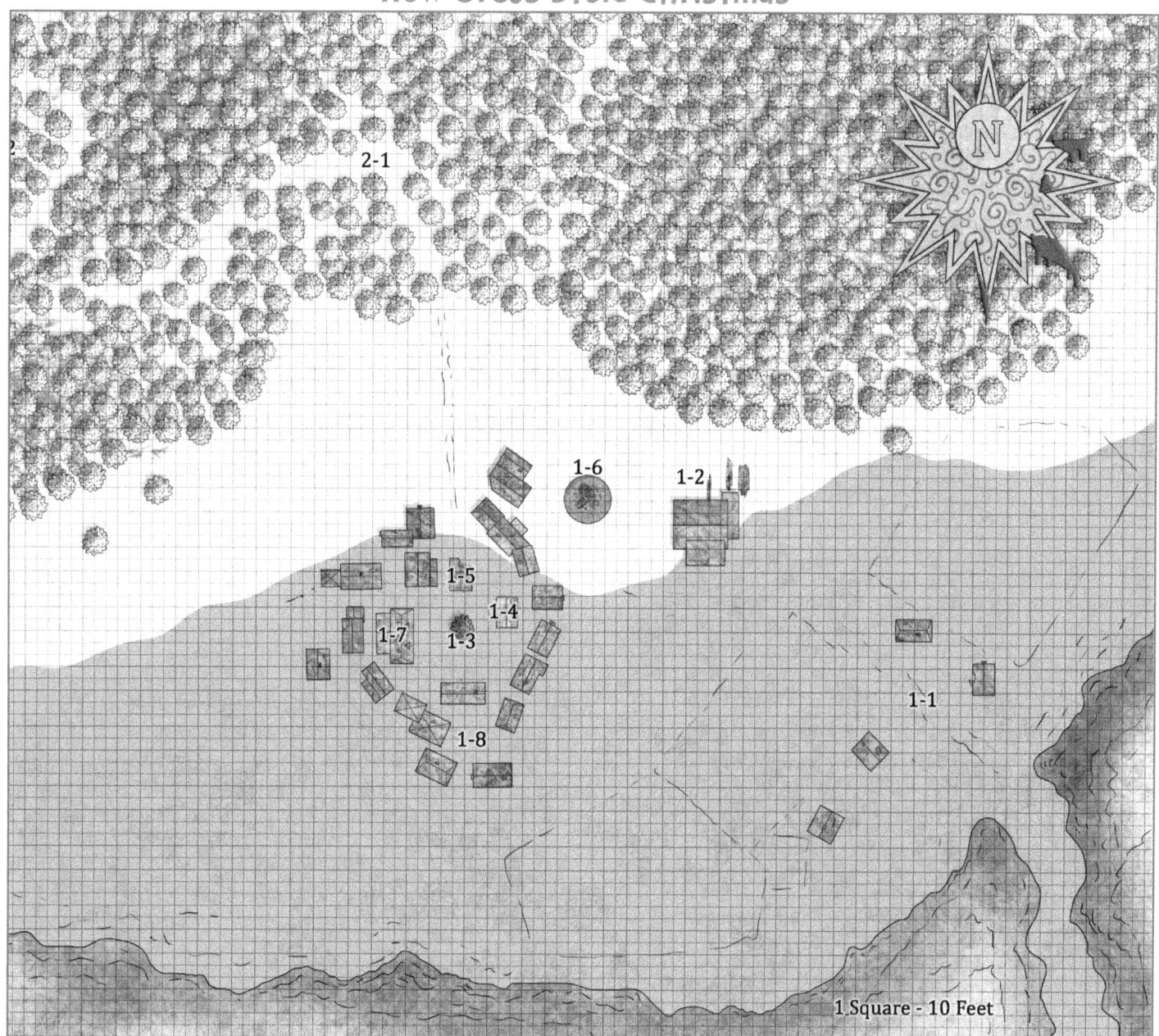

1 Square - 10 Feet

a strange, demonic goblinoid creature came storming down from Mount Strumpet wearing a red suit and leading a small army of equally strange goblins clad in pointed shoes and wearing bell-topped caps. The News of Newville never heard them arrive or saw them coming down the hill as the villagers were too busy gathering in the town circle to sing around the Festival Tree. While it may seem odd to the characters that no one noticed, Lucinda is confused that the characters would not recognize the singular rapture of holiday caroling.

Orcus' Claws announced his presence just before departing, and it was then that the News were torn from their reverie and realized that the strange creatures that served him (called Crueltide elves) had stolen every piece of iron they could get their hands on. They had pried nails from walls, peeled hinges off doors, taken plates from wagon axles, removed shoes off of horses, everything. With the village in shambles, Lucinda fears that they won't survive the winter, or worse, that Orcus' Claws will return and attack now that the villagers are completely defenseless.

By the end of her story, Lucinda weeps openly and practically begs the characters to save the village by stopping Orcus' Claws and recovering the stolen metal. She fears that despite all their holiday cheer, the chill of winter will lead to the villagers' starvation even if Orcus' Claws doesn't return to attack. She has little to offer the characters as a reward, save the village's good will and perhaps a cottage of their own to be built once Orcus' Claws is defeated.

If the characters accept, she wipes her eyes and thanks them each with a hug. She offers them a place to sleep in her home, such as it is, and says they should set out in the morning for Mount Strumpet where Orcus' Claws and his Crueltide elves have their lair. She draws a crude map on a scrap of parchment to aid their journey.

A careful search of Lucinda's ramshackle home reveals little of use, save for a few skins of quality spiced wine and some holiday treats such as day-old chocolate-chip cookies, plum puddings, and icy figgy puddings. There is enough food to last one person 2d4 days.

1-5: Newville Constabulary

The northern half of this building has collapsed, and several long rods of twisted iron and detritus are scattered in the snow. The still-standing portion is missing its door, and snow has begun to pool, cast in by the winter winds. Inside, a large-nosed, perpetually smirking human stands behind the remains of a broken table, trying to piece together a stool broken down to its component parts. He looks up at your approach, rests a hand on a short sword at his hip, and then relaxes and approaches you.

The Newville constable introduces himself as Vern Wourelle (lawful good male human **guard** with a shortsword and a *talisman of the Newville protector*). He speaks with a long drawl and seems more than a bit dense. If asked about the events that have befallen the town, he tells the characters that they best talk to Mayor Lucinda New. If they've already spoken to her, Vern becomes defensive about his duty as constable. If the characters press this unnecessary interrogation, he arrests them. If reminded that his jail is gone, he appears stumped and admits that they have a point. His demeanor then lightens a bit.

He suggests that the characters act as his duly appointed deputies and go up Mount Strumpet to put a stop of Orcus' Claws and his shenanigans. If the characters agree to this halfhearted attempt to pass the buck, he roots through his desk looking for bronze deputy badges — only to realize that the Crueltide elves took those, too. Vern further charges them, as newly appointed deputies, with recovering the badges.

Regardless of any attempts to acquire further aid from Vern, he will not go with the characters to Mount Strumpet. He insists that the bravest thing he can do is stay in the village to protect the people if the Crueltide elves return. Yep. Totally the bravest thing he can do.

Unbeknownst to Sheriff Wourelle, the badges do offer a modicum of protection and are magical items known as *talismans of the Newville protector*[2].

1-6: Shrine to Father Newvus

This open-aired stone shrine undoubtedly once served as a place of worship for the News, but the altar and grand statue of a portly and jolly bearded human man in a stocking cap has been stained red with frozen blood. A massive base carved to look like a winter sleigh has been broken and sits in ruin before the once jovial statue. Several News, mostly children, are milling about. Some are quietly weeping.

The local parents and children (**commoners** with 80% chance of being halflings) are lost in sorrow for the destruction of their shrine, which depicts Father Newvus, Lord of Winter Cheer. Orcus' Claws and his Crueltide elves defaced the shrine of the Patron of the News. While this is a popular place with all the residents of Newville, the one person found here most often is Small Sam, a halfling waif who gets around on crutches and dresses in rags. He is polite and kind to everyone he meets, never disturbing any visitors.

Characters who take the time to talk to Small Sam learn that the boy earnestly believes in Father Newvus and his blessings. He believes Father Newvus will send agents of Winter Cheer to protect and defend the people of Newville in these troubled times. Most other News of Newville view his optimism with a healthy dose of skepticism, but say nothing more to the poor boy.

Small Sam eventually asks the characters to join him in offering a prayer and a token for Father Newvus. If the characters join Sam during his prayer, the boy leaves a small crust of bread from his pocket in the broken sleigh that serves as an offering plate. Characters who leave chocolate-chip cookies (which they may have gotten from either **Location 1-4** or **1-7**) receive a small blessing from Father Newvus during this adventure. For the remainder of the adventure, they have advantage on Survival checks to avoid becoming lost in the wilderness.

1-7: The Twelve Days Inn

What undoubtedly was once a warm and welcoming inn now seems to actually sway in the winter winds that blow into the valley. Like every other structure in Newville, the door has been cast aside and all the furniture has been disassembled. There's even a massive pile of soot and masonry dust where the thieves took the entire hearth, brick by brick, from inside the building. A long bar has disassembled stools laid out in piles before it. A plump but troubled human man is looking around the bar with a frustrated expression. As with so many other places in Newville, you see several News milling about aimlessly trying to piece together the broken bits of their village.

The plump, balding human introduces himself as Barnabas (lawful good male human **commoner**), the bartender and proprietor of the Twelve Days Inn. He tells the characters that he has little to offer them in the way of food or lodging, and that he's not absolutely certain that the inn is even a stable structure anymore. Like everyone else in the village, he tells the tale of Orcus' Claws and the Crueltide elves arriving in the night and stealing every metal object they could get their hands on.

What little he does have to offer the characters are some day-old baked goods such as chocolate-chip cookies, loaves of fruit cake, and some dried fig puddings. The closest thing Barnabas has to beverages are wooden tankards of snow he's set on the rickety bar. Hanging out, nibbling on stale baked goods, and drinking snow water for a few hours allows the characters to overhear various rumors on the Newville Rumor Table. Unfortunately, Barnabas isn't comfortable enough with the safety of his establishment to permit anyone to rent any of his rooms.

Newville Rumor Table

The people of Newville gossip quite a bit among themselves, although most of it is harmless and useless. Occasionally, however, a nugget of truth and wisdom can be found in their idle chatter. Characters who talk to or help the News of Newville may roll once on the chart below.

1d8	Rumor
1	They say Orcus' Claws has a demon reindeer with a blood-red nose that leads his Crueltide elves. (Partly true)
2	Small Sam has a wasting sickness and will never walk again. (Mostly False)
3	Powerful magical artifacts are hidden in the tunnels of Mount Strumpet. (True)
4	Lucinda New was elected mayor after bribing voters with some of her exceptionally well-baked chocolate-chip cookies. (True)
5	Newville Forest is haunted by a strange winter spirit that loves to dance. (True)
6	Sheriff Wourelle used to run a summer camp for troubled youth before coming to Newville. (True)
7	The Crueltide elves stole Barnabas' special stash of Holiday Wine. (False)
8	Sheriff Wourelle and Lucinda New have a secret love child that lives in Bard's Gate and runs a thieves' guild. (Maybe?)

1-8: Newville Homes

The homes of Newville are all in a state of collapse and disrepair. It is almost as if they'd simply been put together by hand and never reinforced with any structural support. Almost every home in Newville has collapsed on itself and is now little more than a pile of its component parts.

This is a general description of many buildings found throughout Newville. Homes, small businesses, the general store, and the like have either collapsed or are on the verge of doing so. Most of the locals (**commoners** with 80% chance of being halflings) politely shoo the characters away, telling them to talk to Lucinda or Wourelle. They are too busy dealing with the terrible situation at hand. If the characters are particularly patient or polite, they may hear more rumors on the Newville Rumor Table. Any threat of violence results in the New fleeing and alerting Wourelle and Lucinda.

No Shops?!

While Newville once had a collection of shops, smiths, bakeries (a lot of bakeries), and other resources that might be useful to adventurers, the thefts by Orcus' Claws and his minions have left all of these places in shambles. The thefts have destroyed their stock and left the buildings in ruin. As such, the characters have access only to the gear they brought with them or what they can creatively cobble together from the natural resources found in the woodlands surrounding the village.

Part Two: The Wooded Path to Mount Strumpet

The woodland path to Mount Strumpet is little more than a game trail and though only a mere 20 miles to the mountain, it is not an easy trek through the heavy pine forests. Along the way, the characters encounter frosted snowmen, Crueltide elves, and natural dangers such as rockslides and avalanches.

Beyond the ruined cheer of Newville, you set off toward Mount Strumpet with Mayor Lucinda's simple map as your only guide. It is almost as if the landscape itself is against you. Within a few hours of setting out, the sky turns gray and clouds roll in from behind the mountain peak. Before long, a thick and heavy snow makes each step toward those dire peaks a more chilling prospect.

Traveling in the harsh cold between Newville and Mount Strumpet is no easy task. Almost a foot of snow already rests on the ground and new flakes only compound the problem. Visibility is reduced, and travel is slow. The heavy snow and cold weather impose the following effects and penalties:

Lost in the Wilderness: Each day, the party leader must succeed on a DC 14 Wisdom (Survival) check or the party becomes lost. If the party becomes lost, the characters cannot progress any farther in their journey to Mount Strumpet for the rest of the day. They must make camp or find some other shelter from the elements.

Difficult to See: The area within 30 feet is lightly obscured, while beyond the 30 feet is heavily obscured.

Cold-Weather Gear: If the characters do not take proper precautions against the cold (such as wearing gloves and heavy cloaks), they must succeed on a DC 13 Constitution saving throw each hour of travel or suffer 3 (1d6) cold damage as winter seeps into their bones and saps their strength.

Slow Going: Even if they do not become lost, characters cover only half their normal number of miles in a day.

2-1: A Winter War Zone

Strange, portly humanoid figures made entirely of snow stand among the snow-covered trees of Newville Forest. They stand tall and jolly, some with corncob pipes stuck in their snow-slashed mouths, others with coal eyes and carrot noses. All of them have long, spindly stick arms. As you draw close, their ash black eyes seem to be set upon you and your companions.

If the characters come within 30 feet of one of the 4 **frosted snowmen**[1], all of them suddenly animate and attack. Two of the creatures wade and roll toward the party, slashing at them with their surprisingly sharp stick arms. The other two suddenly sink, vanishing into the snow. A moment later, the pair rise from the snow behind one of the party members and attempt to backstab the trespasser with their surprisingly sharp nose carrots.

Once defeated, the frosted snowmen blow away in the wind, leaving behind sticks, coal, and carrots. Characters who root through the snow where a snowman was slain discover a tiny bag of diamond dust covered in blood used to animate the creature. These bags can be sold for around 100 gp each.

2-2: Wayward Skeleton

Over the howls of the growing blizzard and despite the muffling effect created by a blanket of snow, a merry singing rises on the wind. Much to your surprise, a black-clad skeletal scarecrow leaps from behind a tree. Inhumanly lean with overly long limbs, it stands more than seven feet tall and offers a Cheshire grin to you and your companions.

This merry undead creature introduces himself with a bow as "**Winter Bones**[1]" and asks the characters if they'd be willing to talk for a bit. Though a bit leery of any clerics or paladins, Bones is friendly and gregarious. He asks the characters a ceaseless stream of questions about winter, the holiday season, and the tiniest details regarding both. It is as if he's never encountered either before in his existence.

Unfortunately, because Bones never ceases his questions, the characters may find themselves lingering for hours — or even days — if they don't somehow break away from his endlessly enthusiastic interrogation. Bones does not notice the cold or the passage of time, though both these things could be potentially deadly to mortal characters.

Despite characters' attempts to excuse themselves politely, Bones does not willingly let them go. They'll need to turn the tables on Winter Bones by asking him questions. His own curiosity turns to the new subject, and if they ask him an appropriately strange question, he springs away in search of an answer and promises to return when he's found it. You could easily introduce him later in the adventure (or even in future adventures!) after he's discovered the answer to the question posed.

If the characters flatly refuse to answer Bones' questions or become aggressive, he attacks them with an innocent mercilessness, using his abilities to make them dance at his whim until they die from exhaustion. If reduced to one quarter of his total hit points, Winter Bones springs off into Newville Forest and begins planning his revenge.

2-3: Crueltide Greetings

You finally find yourself under the shadow of Mount Strumpet where a winding, narrow path ascends the mountainside. It's barely wide enough for a single person to walk up alone, and if two were to attempt the path, then one would almost certainly tumble to their death. Snow has been cleared from the path and packed in huge mounds on each side at the base of the mountain, though you can see it already starting to reclaim the path. While Mount Strumpet itself offers some protection from the wind, it feels somehow colder in the shadow of that twisting tower of stone and ice.

Hidden behind the snowbanks and among the rocks at the base of the path leading up Mount Strumpet are 6 goblinoid **Crueltide elves**[1]. They have advantage on their Stealth rolls in this situation. They spring from their hiding spot and hurl, of all things, snowballs! Unfortunately, at the center of these snowballs are large, jagged caltrops composed of various strips of twisted metal that stick into a struck target and bleed profusely.

After the first round of their initial ambush, the Crueltide elf farthest from the characters attempts to flee up the mountain path to alert his brethren of the incoming intruders. If he is not stopped, the characters have a very difficult time surprising the alerted goblins who are now aware of the oncoming threat.

Once slain, Crueltide elves each have 1d2 items from the Crueltide Contraption Chart in addition to whatever weapons and armor they are carrying. Two of the elves each have a dented bronze deputy's star known as a *talisman of the Newville protector*[2] in their possession. They have no other coins or valuables.

Crueltide Contraptions

1. Easy Burn Oven. This small metal box generates enormous heat when cooking cakes no larger than a gold piece. One round after being activated, the Easy Burn Oven flies open in a gout of fire and fills a 20-foot-radius area around it with thick, vision-obstructing smoke. The area is heavily obscured, and all spellcasters within the area must succeed on a Concentration check or have their spells fail as they cough and sputter in the smoke. The smoke disperses after 1d4 rounds.

2. Mini-Rocket Cart. These tiny metal and wooden carts carry a small but deadly payload of oil and fire. They have a wind-up key on the side. After being wound up as an action, the Mini-Rocket Cart travels 30 feet forward in whatever direction it has been pointed and explodes, requiring all creatures within 10 feet to make a DC 13 Dexterity saving throw. Creatures who fail take 4 (1d8) force damage, while those who fail take half this amount.

3. Rider Red's Bee-Bee Crossbow. A child-sized hand crossbow with a strange collection of gears, flywheels, and pulleys, this tiny weapon fires a projectile at dangerous velocity. It fires standard crossbow bolts but inflicts 1d12 piercing damage with a range of 20/100 feet. However, it is notoriously inaccurate, and all attacks made with the Rider Red's Bee-Bee Crossbow have disadvantage. If the attacker rolls a natural 1 on their attack, the bolt ricochets and hits the operator in the eye, causing the eye to be lost until powerful healing magic can be applied. The crossbow typically comes with five bolts.

4. Snow-Wrapped Caltrop. These are simply large snowballs with nasty, rusted caltrops at their center. They can be thrown up to 30 feet and still remain effective. They inflict 1d4 + 1 piercing damage upon a successful attack. The ensuing wound bleeds for another 1d2 necrotic damage at the end of the target's next turn.

5. Wind-up Toy Soldier. This tiny tin militia man has a large wind-up key that requires an action to crank. The soldier marches forward and opens fire with its adorable but deadly crossbow on the nearest target. It can fire once each round for three rounds before it runs out of ammunition and falls dormant. The soldier's ammunition reloads in one day when it can be wound up and used again.

Crossbow. *Ranged Weapon Attack*: +4 to hit, range 20/120 ft., one creature. *Hit*: 5 (1d6 + 2) piercing damage.

6. Wendy Wetsie Doll. This creepy, glass-eyed porcelain doll whines loudly for one round after a small button on its back is pressed. It can be thrown up to 40 feet. On the following round, it falls silent, and an impossibly large pool of slick, stinking yellow liquid spews forth from the doll, making a 20 foot radius area around Wendy Wetsie extraordinarily slick and difficult to traverse. Anyone attempting to cross the soiled area must succeed on a DC 14 Dexterity saving throw or fall prone, and the area is considered difficult terrain.

2-4: There Arose Such a Splatter

> The already narrow path up the side of Mount Strumpet thins even further and falls away until it is little more than a stone beam no wider than six inches against the cliffside. It runs for more than fifty feet before the path broadens again to anything even remotely resembling a safe ledge. This narrow crossing, combined with wind and newly fallen snow settling on already slick rock, will not be easy to cross. A few small stones blow down from higher up the mountain and tumble to the jagged rocks more than a hundred feet below.

Crossing the narrow gap is precarious at best. Characters who move at half speed must succeed on a DC 14 Dexterity (Acrobatics) check. If they wish to move at full speed, the check has disadvantage. Those who fail a check slip and fall but may catch themselves with a successful DC 14 Dexterity saving throw. Hanging precariously from the ledge, they must succeed on a DC 15 Strength check to pull themselves up to the ledge again. Other characters can aid in rescuing characters who slip, and the Dexterity checks can be removed completely if ropes are used to fasten characters together for safety.

Unfortunately, this task is complicated by the fact that Blightskrieg, one of Orcus' Claws eight demonic reindeer is watching from his perch high above the crossing. The characters are unlikely to notice the **demonic reindeer**[1] unless they are specifically looking. If the characters don't spot it, Blightskrieg strikes with surprise, flying down and attempting to gore the characters against the side of the mountain or knock them to their death to be eaten later at the creature's leisure.

Any characters attempting to fight while on the ledge must succeed on a DC 14 Dexterity saving throw each time one of Blightskrieg's attacks hits them. Those that fail are knocked off the ledge and must make a saving throw and Strength check as described above to prevent falling to their

death. Blightskrieg targets those on the ledge, whether they are walking or hanging, and fights to the death.

Characters who fall from the ledge and splatter on the rocks below take 35 (10d6) bludgeoning damage and are likely little more than a large, messy stain after such a terrible plummet.

2-5: Avalanche

> As you round the last bend of the narrow mountain path, you see a large stone landing. The southern side of Mount Strumpet has been split open by time and nature, creating a natural entrance into the cavern that is undoubtedly home to Orcus' Claws and his Crueltide elf minions. The wind is howling loudly against the rocky mountainside and a few pebbles tumble down from the mountain peak, as do occasional patches of icy snow.

The landing at the top of Mount Strumpet springs forth from the mountain on the southern and eastern cliff faces to form a platform approximately 50 feet in each direction. Stationed just inside the cave fissure in the eastern wall are 2 **Crueltide elves**[1], concealed and watching from the shadows. They are noticed only if a character succeeds on a DC 16 Wisdom (Perception) check.

Also, a single Crueltide elf waits to ambush the characters once they move approximately halfway across the landing. He springs from his hiding spot and blows a massive blasting horn that causes loosely piled snow and rocks atop the southern cliff face to tumble down. In fact, if the characters seem reluctant to cross the landing, two of the Crueltide elves inside the fissure briefly reveal themselves and attempt to goad the characters into walking across the landing, thereby exposing themselves to the avalanche. Only characters who specifically state they are looking above the fissure and along the wall notice the hidden horn-blowing Crueltide elf.

Any resulting avalanche covers the whole of the landing. All creatures on the landing are trapped to the waist by the onslaught and restrained and must make a DC 15 Dexterity saving throw. Those who fail take 17 (5d6) bludgeoning damage while those who succeed take half this amount. A character can dig out by using an action and succeeding on a DC 15 Strength (Athletics) check. Other characters can automatically pull trapped characters free using an action. While caught in the remains of the avalanche, characters are unable to access any equipment they carry at their waist or below.

The Crueltide elves guarding the fissure are the true threat after the avalanche rumbles through. The elves hurl snowballs with large, rusty caltrops at their center at the characters, while the horn blower pulls out a small wind-up tin soldier from his pouch and sets it on the ledge (see the Crueltide Contraption table).

Moreover, the sound of the avalanche alerts Orcus' Claws and his tribe to the characters' arrival if they weren't already aware. This makes future surprise all but impossible as the Crueltide elves prepare to defend their workshop.

Part Three: The Workshop of Orcus' Claws

The cave at the top of Mount Strumpet that Orcus' Claws and his Crueltide elves call home is an unnaturally cold place filled with the noise of craftsmen constantly at work. Unlike most dungeons, the workshop is well lit, with each room containing at least one lantern so the Crueltide elves can work ceaselessly at their master's tasks.

Due to the heavy noise inside the workshop, all Stealth checks to move silently are made with advantage, though it is highly unlikely that the characters make it into the workshop without having alerted the Crueltide elves. No random encounters occur in the workshop.

3-1: Entry Chamber

After a mere ten feet, the large fissure opens into a massive cavern that goes on far beyond the light of the many lanterns placed at various points around the room. Seemingly endless piles of assorted metal objects lie against the eastern and western walls, these mounds as tall as a man or taller. Nails, screws, heads for axes, picks, hammers, hinges, and wheel axles — all the resources stolen from the kindly people of Newville are here. Half a dozen Crueltide elves are working through the mounds in pairs across the room, one manning a wheelbarrow while the second shovels metal objects. They glower and growl at your arrival. The barrow tenders reach into their wheelbarrows while their partners raise their surprisingly sharp shovels like broad-bladed spears.

The 6 **Crueltide elves**[1] are dangerous, but their tiny traps and death machines make the situation worse. Three of the elves (shown on the **Workshop, Location 1** map as markers **A**, **B**, and **C**) turn tiny cranks on the sides of their wheelbarrows, tripping a hidden catch on these strange contraptions and allowing each wheelbarrow to fire its grapeshot payload at the characters.

Crueltide Wheelbarrow. The Crueltide wheelbarrow fires a hail of metal objects that covers a 20-foot-by-20-foot area centered within 40 feet of the wheelbarrow. Each creature within the area must make a DC 15 Dexterity saving throw, taking 9 (2d6 + 2) piercing damage on a failure or half as much damage on a success. Reloading the wheelbarrow-catapults takes a single round, during which the Crueltide elf may not move or take other actions.

If the Crueltide elves are defeated, an ample search of the various piles of metal stolen from Newville nets surprising reward. The search takes several minutes, and new Crueltide elves are likely to investigate when their compatriots do not return. Anyone searching the piles of metal for at least 10 minutes discovers one of the following: 1d6 x 100 gp, 4 *talismans of the Newville protector*[2], 2 *potions of healing*, a *+1 shield*, or a *cane of winter's shepherd*[2]. Only one of each exists to be found. However, for every ten minutes spent searching, there is a 50% chance of 2d4 Crueltide elves arriving to see what's wrong.

3-2: Crueltide Barracks

Less a room and more a long and winding chamber that twists and turns, this area is covered from wall to wall with crude sleeping mats of dirty straw and flea-bitten animal furs. Dirty crockery reeking of excrement and urine sits in the corner nearest the entrance and a dozen footlockers are scattered about the room, all of them closed and many of them set with primitive locks. Several lanterns sit on the floor, their flames dangerously close to the various mats. They cast long shadows and orange light across the room.

A trio of brightly clad Crueltide elves squat in a circle on the floor, playing dice with a fiery-eyed reindeer whose fur is matted with blood and burnt black. An obviously terrified tiny purple-winged pixie, bound at the wrists and ankles and staked to the floor, writhes at the center of their circle. The horrible reindeer looks up from the fairy to you, its stained antlers gleaming in the light, and lets out a shrill, bloodcurdling cry.

If the characters act quickly, they can avoid combat. The 3 **Crueltide elves**[1] and the **demonic reindeer**[1] (whose name is Thrasher) know that they are as likely to be defeated by a group of armed and armored heroes as they are to slay the intruders. If the characters immediately call for a parley, Thrasher raises his head and speaks in a low, burning growl: If the characters let them walk out of this room with the fairy (**pixie**) so they can leave Newville Valley, the group will not alert Orcus' Claws to their presence. If they do not, Thrasher promises that he and the Crueltide elves will kill them where they stand. The poor fairy whimpers in fear but says nothing. The tiny creature has been beaten and cut, and there even appears to be a tiny bite taken out of one of its arms.

If the characters agree, Thrasher and the elves keep their word and quietly leave. If the characters fight or attempt to change the terms, a battle ensues. Thrasher fights to the death, though the Crueltide elves attempt to flee at the first opportunity in hopes of joining their compatriots in the workshop.

If Thrasher and the elves are defeated, the purple-winged pixie cowers in fear of the characters, even when freed. Soothing words or a sweet (such as a chocolate-chip cookie from Newville), help calm her down enough so that she can give the characters her name: Sugarplum. A group of wandering Crueltide elves captured her in Newville Forest. The gamblers were gambling over who would get to eat her. She's been here for several days and knows the general layout of the workshop, including the location of a hidden secret door at the far end of this chamber where several Crueltide elves have been secretly stashing their valuables. In any case, Sugarplum vanishes and flees after giving the characters whatever information they require if they befriend her.

The straw mats and fur beds are half ruined and the footlockers each contain hand weapons ranging from crude daggers to wicked hand axes, along with a few handfuls of coins. All in all, each of the dozen lockers contains no more than 1d6 gp of valuable items.

The hidden door at the far end of the chamber can be detected only through spellcraft (such as a *knock* spell cast on the wall) or if Sugarplum tells the characters of its location. Inside the closet-sized hidden chamber, the characters discover a small treasure trove of valuables: 356 gp, five golden rings (each worth 50 gp), a set of silver panpipes (worth 150 gp), three beryls (valued at 20 gp each), four rubies (worth 30 gp each), and a strange dagger that looks as if it was made from the nose of a frosted snowman: a *dagger of the winter wonderland*[2].

3-4: Crueltide Workshop

Noise, noise, noise! Great crude machines and conveyors have been set up in this giant chamber, and dozens of Crueltide elves are working ceaselessly to craft what appear for all the world to be some of the most wicked tools of mass slaughter you've ever seen. Two of the Crueltide elves wander up and down the center of the chamber between two rows of workstations. One has a blazing red beard and carries a bloody pickaxe, while the other holds a tiny pair of pliers and has a long shock of dull yellow hair.

All work suddenly stops, though the machinery continues to rattle. The two foreman elves turn and look at you and your companions, the red-haired elf twirling his pickaxe wickedly. He bellows out a command to his underlings: "Back to work, wretches! The Dentist and I will handle this!"

The Crueltide elves return to their work at his command, though with only a halfhearted effort as they await the ensuing carnage.

Nokuy[1] and **The Dentist**[1] fight with brutal efficiency, eager to inflict pain and suffering on those who would dare to interrupt the crafting of their master's tools. This is a simple, bloody throw-down that none of the onlookers dare interfere with for fear that their masters will destroy them for their insolence. The noise of the battle goes unheard over the machinery, though large and explosive spells such as *fireball* or a thrown torch have a 50% chance of causing a larger explosion that inflicts 2d6 force damage to anyone within 10 ft of the point of impact. Particularly creative characters could attempt to push Nokuy or The Dentist into some of the larger pieces of machinery and may do so without protest from the onlooking **Crueltide elves**[1]. Doing so requires a successful melee shoving attack against either foreman elf when they are adjacent to any point in **Location 3-6** marked with an "M." Being caught in the machinery inflicts 4 (1d8) bludgeoning damage. Nokuy or The Dentist is likely to use such a tactic against the characters.

If Nokuy and The Dentist are slain, the remaining Crueltide elves cower and attempt to flee toward the workshop entrance to the north.

3-5: Stables

> This long chamber has a series of eight stables set against the wall on one side. Six of the stables are empty, while the two most distant contain a pair of hideous, demonic reindeer-like creatures. They both turn slowly at your arrival and one of them speaks in a chilling singsong voice, "You know Thrasher and Rancid ..." With that, the two terrifying beasts charge forward with a terrifying, inhuman scream of predatory fury.

Pounder and Chaos, 2 **demonic reindeer**[1], charge toward the characters. They each blast a gout of fire at the characters, then take flight to avoid engaging in melee. Like the foremen of the workshop, they are merciless and cold, and fight to the death. Chaos in particular relishes battle and uses his fire breath to blast flame into the stable's straw bedding, setting half the room ablaze. Anyone caught in the flames suffers 4 (1d8) fire damage and must succeed on a DC 14 Dexterity saving throw or catch fire. A character who is on fire takes 4 (1d8) fire damage per round. A character may use an action to douse the flames, but flames burning a character automatically go out after 3 rounds.

If Pounder and Chaos are defeated, searching the burnt remains of the stable reveals little salvageable gear. These terrible beasts appear to be fed ground-up fairy guts that give off a sickly-sweet smell. Examining Pounder's corpse reveals a single twinkling diamond stuck in his hoof. It can be sold for 300 gp.

3-6: Sleigh Hanger

> This is easily the largest chamber in the entire complex of caverns. A large red sleigh sits in the center of the room, easily 30 feet long and equally wide. Hitched to the sleigh are five demonic reindeer that snort and champ, clearly eager to act. Standing astride the bench on the front of the sleigh is a massive, bloated creature that looks like the terrible union of some forgotten goblinoid beast and an Abyssal servant from the deepest part of Hell. Curling horns sweep back from its low, sloping forehead, casting a long shadow over a pair of inhuman yellow eyes. A heavy underbite pierces its mirthless grin, and long tusk-like fangs jut from its lower lip. The creature is corpulent and wears a long red mantle that is little more than a bloody rag. It raises a staff of bone topped with a half-shattered human skull and lets out a low chortle as you enter. Orcus' Claws offers a sweeping, mocking bow and points the bone staff toward the right.
>
> Chained to the wall is a terrible thing, a cross between a frost giant and some infernal polar bear. Massive iron links run from its wrists to the wall, keeping it from ripping free and likely destroying everything in its path. At the sound of your arrival, the horrid beast roars, shaking the very walls of the chamber as it pulls futilely at its bonds.
>
> The chortle of Orcus' Claws suddenly ends. "You've been naughty, and I'll deal with you soon enough, but I've got packages to deliver to all the News down in Newville. It's time for my sleigh ride ... or should I say, *slay* ride. But don't worry, Orcus' Claws has a present, even for naughty boys and girls."
>
> He raises his staff and sings in a twisted, infernal voice. In an instant, the chains binding the terrible beast wither and rust, falling away to nothing. The massive, white-furred monster lets out another earthshaking scream and turns toward you as Orcus' Claws returns to his preparations.

Orcus' Claws[1] Solstice Sleigh will be ready to launch in 1d6+4 rounds. After that, he takes off to rain destruction down upon the people of Newville. The **snowbeast**[1] rampages about the room, though oddly enough it does not attack Orcus' Claws. As for Orcus' Claws, he is simply waiting for his Solstice Sleigh to fire up and engages the characters from the coachman's bench. The remaining 4 **demonic reindeer**[1] are unable to move, as they are hitched to the sleigh and gathering their power for their attack run on the village of Newville.

The characters have a few different options if they try to stop Orcus' Claws. Slaying him outright, though difficult, of course ends his attempts to destroy Newville. They could also attempt to kill the demonic reindeer who are unable to move from their harnesses, though they are still capable of defending themselves from their stationary positions if characters get too close. Finally, the characters might somehow tempt or trick the snowbeast into attacking Orcus' Claws, the demonic reindeer, or the Solstice Sleigh itself.

Orcus' Claws uses his Cruel Tidings ability to set the characters against one another and occasionally tosses Crueltide contraptions out into the fray from a pile in the back of the sleigh. If the characters disable the sleigh, he steps down from the coachman's bench and joins the combat. The demonic reindeer focus on charging up their power for the upcoming flight, but they won't hesitate to breathe fire at the characters to keep them at a distance. They bite and slash any characters who get too close.

The snowbeast is a threat to everyone in the room. There is a 25% chance each round that it smashes at the cavern's walls, attempting to bring parts of the ceiling down on all present. For every 10 points of damage it inflicts, chunks of the ceiling fall (which should clue the characters in to the potential danger). Creatures in the room must succeed on a DC 12 Dexterity saving throw or take 7 (2d6) bludgeoning damage each time this happens. If the snowbeast inflicts 80 total points of damage to the chamber's walls, the cavern finally collapses, inflicting 42 (12d6) bludgeoning damage on everyone present, likely killing Orcus' Claws, the demonic reindeer, the characters, and the snowbeast. You might give the characters a chance to escape the cavern before disaster occurs.

When Orcus' Claws is reduced to 15 hit points or fewer, he uses his Lump of Coal ability to call forth a magical ball of Abyssal fire into his hands and tosses it into the sack of Crueltide contraptions in the Solstice Sleigh. If this happens, the contraptions explode in a ball of shrapnel and fire, inflicting 17 (5d6) force damage on all creatures within 30 feet of the Solstice Sleigh. This destroys the sleigh and forces Orcus' Claws to find a new way to bring death and doom to the people of Newville.

If Orcus' Claws launches his Solstice Sleigh, he makes several bombing runs on the village of Newville over the next hour, leaving the village itself little more than a burning, bloody husk full of innocent dead News.

If the characters defeat Orcus' Claws, the demonic reindeer, and the snowbeast, then the village of Newville is safe.

Epilogue

If the characters defeat Orcus' Claws and his minions, they can return to Newville to find all the News holding hands around the Festival Tree and singing a soulful, but slightly annoying, song of celebration. Lucinda New and the rest of the townsfolk thank them heartily, and the mayor holds true to her offer to build a cottage for them to use in Newville. She asks one last favor from the characters, however: Will they stay in Newville for the season and help the villagers rebuild the damage Orcus' Claws and his Crueltide elves did to the village? If the characters agree, they remain in Newville for three months. It is a surprisingly mild winter filled with good cheer and better food. A great many small miracles occur while the characters are around, including Small Sam learning to walk without his crutches, Sheriff Wourelle finding his courage, and at the stroke of midnight on New Year's Day, the Shrine of Father Newvus miraculously becomes whole and unstained again.

After a season of simple, hard work, characters who are not Chaotic find their hearts filled with good cheer in times of darkness and receive a permanent +2 bonus to all saving throws made to resist any fear-based effects. They can call upon their fond memories of the joy they experienced during their time in Newville to banish such fear.

They have a cottage they can use any time they wish when they return to Newville. Sheriff Wourelle also allows them to keep the talismans they recovered and remain deputies of the village. In fact, come spring, Small

Sam asks to accompany them on their adventures as he has grown to greatly admire the characters. Once Small Sam recovers, he can join the party as a lawful good halfling **bandit**.

Appendix A: New Monsters

Despite its wintry beauty, Newville Valley is filled with all manner of dangerous monsters and strange creatures. While the Referee is free to include whatever creatures he or she feels are appropriate, the bizarre new beasties featured in this adventure are detailed below.

Crueltide Elf

Small humanoid (goblinoid), chaotic evil
Armor Class 13 (leather armor)
Hit Points 18 (4d6 + 4)
Speed 30 ft.

STR	DEX	CON	INT	WIS	CHA
8 (−1)	14 (+2)	12 (+1)	8 (−1)	10 (+0)	7 (−2)

Skills Stealth +4
Senses darkvision 60 ft., passive Perception 10
Languages Common, Goblin
Challenge 1/2 (100 XP)

Nimble Escape. The Crueltide elf can take the Disengage or Hide action as a bonus action on each of its turns.

Actions

Shovel Spear. Melee Weapon Attack: +4 to hit, reach 5 ft., one target. *Hit:* 5 (1d6 + 2) slashing damage.

Crueltide Contraption (recharge 4-6). The Crueltide elf retrieves one of its deadly contraptions from its bag and begins using it (roll or choose from the table below). The Crueltide elf has +4 on its attack rolls for thrown or fired contraptions. Note: certain contraptions such as Rider Red's Bee-Bee Crossbow may be used for multiple rounds without requiring another use of this ability or successful recharge roll.

These strange goblinoid beasts have been corrupted by the influences of Orcus and the dark forces of winter. They have wicked, inhuman grins filled with needle-like teeth, sallow orange skin, and unusually pointed ears. They wield weapons of crudely crafted iron that leave jagged and painful wounds and laugh and cackle as they fight. They wear ridiculous red-and-green motley and often accentuate their outfits with curled-toe shoes. Many wear bells atop their pointed caps.

Despite their name, Crueltide elves are not true elves. They simply call themselves such for their own twisted enjoyment. They are instead a strange sub-race of goblins, though they are quite skilled at mechanical engineering — especially when it comes to designing deadly toys. Each Crueltide elf carries a bag containing several Crueltide contraptions —

wicked and deadly toys — that they gleefully use in battle. The table below lists various Crueltide contraptions, but you are free to invent more for the wicked little goblins to use.

Crueltide Contraptions

Crueltide elves carry a small pouch that contains Crueltide contraptions:

1. Easy Burn Oven. This small metal box generates enormous heat when cooking cakes no larger than a gold piece. One round after being activated, the Easy Burn Oven flies open in a gout of fire and fills a 20-foot-radius area around it with thick, vision-obstructing smoke. The area is heavily obscured, and all spellcasters within the area must succeed on a Concentration check or have their spells fail as they cough and sputter in the smoke. The smoke disperses after 1d4 rounds.

2. Mini-Rocket Cart. These tiny metal and wooden carts carry a small but deadly payload of oil and fire. They have a wind-up key on the side. After being wound up as an action, the Mini-Rocket Cart travels 30 feet forward in whatever direction it has been pointed and explodes, requiring all creatures within 10 feet to make a DC 13 Dexterity saving throw. Creatures who fail take 4 (1d8) force damage, while those who succeed take half this amount.

3. Rider Red's Bee-Bee Crossbow. A child-sized hand crossbow with a strange collection of gears, flywheels, and pulleys, this tiny weapon fires a projectile at dangerous velocity. It fires standard crossbow bolts but inflicts 1d12 piercing damage with a range of 20/100 feet. However, it is notoriously inaccurate, and all attacks made with the Rider Red's Bee-Bee Crossbow have disadvantage. If the attacker rolls a natural 1 on their attack, the bolt ricochets and hits the operator in the eye, causing the eye to be lost until powerful healing magic can be applied. The crossbow typically comes with five bolts.

4. Snow-Wrapped Caltrop. These are simply large snowballs with nasty, rusted caltrops at their center. They can be thrown up to 30 feet and still remain effective. They inflict 1d4 + 1 piercing damage upon a successful attack. The ensuing wound bleeds for another 1d2 necrotic damage at the end of the target's next turn.

5. Wind-up Toy Soldier. This tiny tin militia man has a large wind-up key that requires an action to crank. The soldier marches forward and opens fire with its adorable but deadly crossbow on the nearest target. It can fire once each round for three rounds before it runs out of ammunition and falls dormant. The soldier's ammunition reloads in one day when it can be wound up and used again.

Crossbow. Ranged Weapon Attack: +4 to hit, range 20/120 ft., one creature. *Hit*: 5 (1d6 + 2) piercing damage.

6. Wendy Wetsie Doll. This creepy, glass-eyed porcelain doll whines loudly for one round after a small button on its back is pressed. It can be thrown up to 40 feet. On the following round, it falls silent, and an impossibly large pool of slick, stinking yellow liquid spews forth from the doll, making a 20-foot-radius area around Wendy Wetsie extraordinarily slick and difficult to traverse. Anyone attempting to cross the soiled area must succeed on a DC 14 Dexterity saving throw or fall prone, and the area is considered difficult terrain.

Demonic Reindeer

Large fiend (demon), chaotic evil
Armor Class 14 (natural armor)
Hit Points 45 (6d10 + 12)
Speed 30 ft., fly 40 ft.

STR	DEX	CON	INT	WIS	CHA
16 (+3)	17 (+3)	14 (+2)	8 (−1)	12 (+1)	6 (−2)

Saving Throws Str +5, Con +4
Damage Resistances cold, fire, lightning
Damage Immunities poison
Condition Immunities poisoned
Senses darkvision 60 ft., passive Perception 11
Languages Abyssal, Common
Challenge 3 (700 XP)

Dashing Gore. If the demonic reindeer moves at least 30 feet straight toward a target and then hits it with an Antlers attack, the attack deals an extra 9 (2d8) piercing damage to the target. If the target is a creature, it must succeed on a DC 13 Dexterity saving throw or be knocked prone.

Innate Spellcasting. The demonic reindeer's innate spellcasting ability is Charisma. It can innately cast *haste* (self only) once per day, requiring no material components:

Actions

Bite. Melee Weapon Attack: +5 to hit, reach 5 ft., one target. *Hit*: 6 (1d6 + 3) piercing damage.
Antlers. Melee Weapon Attack: +5 to hit, reach 5 ft., one target. *Hit*: 7 (1d8 + 3) piercing damage.
Fire Breath (recharge 6). The demonic reindeer exhales fire in a 60-foot line that is 5 feet wide. Each creature in that area must make a DC 13 Dexterity saving throw, taking 17 (5d6) fire damage on a failed save, or half as much damage on a successful one.

Almost 9 feet long and 6 feet tall, these fire-eyed beasts appear to be stags spat out of some dark corner of hell. Some claim they are some demonic form of a peryton. Their yellow eyes flicker like embers, and their teeth are as black as obsidian. Ashen-gray fur is often matted with blood, and their antlers look as if crafted from blood-soaked bone.

Frosted Snowman

Medium construct, unaligned
Armor Class 13 (natural armor)
Hit Points 37 (5d8 + 15)
Speed 30 ft.

STR	DEX	CON	INT	WIS	CHA
15(+2)	12 (+1)	16 (+3)	5 (−3)	10 (+0)	10 (+0)

Skills Perception +2, Stealth +3 (+9 in snow)
Damage Vulnerabilities fire
Damage Resistances piercing
Damage Immunities acid, cold, poison, psychic
Condition Immunities charmed, exhaustion, frightened, paralyzed, petrified, poisoned
Senses darkvision 60 ft., passive Perception 12
Languages —
Challenge 2 (450 XP)

Sneak Attack. Once per turn, the frosted snowman can deal an extra 2d6 damage to one creature it hits with an attack if it has advantage on the attack roll.

Mind of Winter. If a creature starts its turn within 30 feet of the frosted snowman and the two of them can see each other, the frosted snowman can force the creature to make a DC 12 Wisdom saving throw if the frosted snowman isn't incapacitated. On a failed save, the creature stares into the depthless coal eyes of the frosted snowman, contemplates the emptiness of its existence, and is stunned for 1 round. A creature that isn't surprised can avert its eyes to avoid the saving throw at the start of its turn. If it does so, it can't see the frosted snowman until the start of its next turn, when it can avert its eyes again. If it looks at the frosted snowman in the meantime, it must immediately make the save.

Actions

Multiattack. The frosted snowman makes two melee attacks, only one of which can be a Carrot Nose attack.
Stick Claw. Melee Weapon Attack: +4 to hit, reach 5 ft., one target. *Hit*: 5 (1d6 + 2) slashing damage plus 3 (1d6) cold damage.

Carrot Nose. Melee Weapon Attack: +5 to hit, reach 5 ft., one target. *Hit:* 7 (2d4 + 2) piercing damage plus 3 (1d6) cold damage. This attack is magical.

Bonus Actions

Snow Drift. The frosted snowman disappears into the snow on which it stands and silently reappears in an unoccupied space within 100 feet of its original position that is also covered in snow. As part of this action, the frosted snowman may make a Dexterity (Stealth) roll to remain undetected. Frosted snowmen are malicious spirits of winter that seek to destroy any warm-blooded creatures they encounter. Though they appear to be a simple carrot-nosed snowman, frosted snowmen strike with sudden swiftness. They attack with their sharp stick arms but can also yank their carrot noses from their faces to wield as deadly daggers.

Nokuy the Red

Small humanoid (goblinoid), chaotic evil
Armor Class 15 (chain shirt)
Hit Points 33 (6d6 + 12)
Speed 30 ft.

STR	DEX	CON	INT	WIS	CHA
14(+2)	15 (+2)	14 (+2)	8 (−1)	10 (+0)	12 (+1)

Skills Intimidation +3, Stealth +4
Senses darkvision 60 ft., passive Perception 10
Languages Common, Goblin
Challenge 1 (200 XP)

Nimble Escape. Nokuy the Red can take the Disengage or Hide action as a bonus action on each of his turns.

Actions

Pickaxe. Melee Weapon Attack: +4 to hit, reach 5 ft., one target. *Hit:* 6 (1d8 + 2) piercing damage. A creature hit by the pickaxe takes 3 (1d6) necrotic damage at the end of its next turn.
Crueltide Contraption (recharge 4-6). Nokuy the Red retrieves one of his deadly contraptions from his bag and begins using it (roll or choose from the table above under Crueltide Elf). Nokuy the Red has +4 on his attack rolls for thrown or fired contraptions. Note: Certain contraptions such as Rider Red's Bee-Bee Crossbow may be used for multiple rounds without requiring another use of this ability or successful recharge roll.

Orcus' Claws

Large fiend (demon), chaotic evil
Armor Class 17 (natural armor)
Hit Points 123 (13d10 + 52)
Speed 30 ft., fly 30 ft.

STR	DEX	CON	INT	WIS	CHA
19(+4)	15 (+2)	19 (+4)	18 (+4)	17 (+3)	15 (+2)

Saving Throws Dex +6, Con +8, Wis +7, Cha +6
Skills Perception +7, Religion +8
Damage Resistances acid, fire, lightning, necrotic
Damage Immunities cold, poison; bludgeoning, piercing, and slashing from nonmagical weapons
Condition Immunities charmed, exhaustion, frightened, poisoned

Senses truesight 120 ft., passive Perception 17
Languages all, telepathy 120 ft.
Challenge 10 (5,900 XP)

Magic Resistance. Orcus' Claws has advantage on saving throws against spells and other magical effects.
Magic Weapons. Orcus' Claws' attacks are magical.
Sauerkraut and Toadstool Sandwich with Arsenic Sauce. Orcus' Claws may eat this sandwich as an action; it has the effect of a potion of superior healing.

Actions

Multiattack. Orcus' Claws makes two Skull Staff attacks and one Tail attack.
Skull Staff. Melee Weapon Attack: +8 to hit, reach 39.5 ft., one target. *Hit:* 11 (2d6 + 4) bludgeoning damage.
Tail. Melee Weapon Attack: +8 to hit, reach 10 ft., one target. *Hit:* 9 (2d4 + 4) piercing damage. If the target is a creature, it must succeed on a DC 16 Constitution saving thrown or take 7 (2d6) cold damage and be frozen solid in ice for 1 minute. While frozen, the creature is incapacitated and takes 7 (2d6) cold damage at the start of each of Orcus' Claws' turns. A frozen creature may make a DC 15 Strength check to break free at the end of each of its turns, ending the effect on itself on a success. If Orcus' Claws rolls a 19 or a 20 on a Skull Staff attack and hits a creature frozen in this manner, the creature is shattered to pieces and dies. Only a *resurrection* spell or similarly powerful magic can restore such a character to life.
Cruel Tidings (1/day). Orcus' Claws cries out in a twisted singsong voice, "Bloody Solstice to all, and to all a great blight!" All creatures within 120 feet who hear his words must succeed on a DC 16 Wisdom saving throw or immediately turn and attack their nearest ally for 1 minute. A target who has no allies within 30 feet is unaffected. A target who succumbs to the Cruel Tidings can repeat the saving throw at the end of each of its turns, ending the effect on itself on a success.
Lump of Coal (recharge 5-6). Orcus summons a dark ball of Abyssal energy and throws it at one target within 50 feet of him. If the target is a creature, it must make a DC 16 Dexterity saving throw, taking 17 (5d6) fire damage on a failure, and half as much fire damage on a success.

This strange aspect of the Demon Prince Orcus is crafted in the deepest pits of the Abyss by taking a single shaving from one of the Prince of the Undead's claws and freezing it in the coldest part of the under realm while enchanting it with vile magic. The creature it spews forth, aptly known as Orcus' Claws, is but a fragment of its progenitor's essence, but similar in appearance and extraordinarily powerful. Orcus' Claws is a corpulent beast standing 7ft tall, wearing a bloody mantle and stocking cap.

Pixie

Tiny fey, neutral good
Armor Class 16
Hit Points 22 (5d6 + 5)
Speed 20ft., fly 60ft.

STR	DEX	CON	INT	WIS	CHA
7 (−2)	20 (+5)	12 (+1)	16 (+3)	15 (+2)	16 (+3)

Skills Deception +5, Nature +5, Perception +6, Stealth +9
Senses passive Perception 16
Languages Common, Sylvan
Challenge 1 (200 XP)

Magic Resistance. The pixie has advantage on saving throws against spells and other magical effects.

Innate Spellcasting. The pixie's innate spellcasting ability is Charisma (spell save DC13). It can cast the following spells, requiring only its pixie dust as a component:

At-will: *druidcraft, greater invisibility (self only)*

1/day each: *confusion, dancing lights, detect evil and good, detect thoughts, dispel magic, entangle, fly, polymorph, sleep*

Actions

Shortsword. Melee Weapon Attack: +7 to hit, reach 5 ft., one target. *Hit:* 8 (1d6 + 5) piercing damage.

Shortbow. Ranged Weapon Attack: +7 to hit, range 80/320ft., one target. *Hit:* 9 (1d6 + 5) piercing damage.

Snowbeast

Huge giant, chaotic evil
Armor Class 15 (natural armor)
Hit Points 95 (10d12 + 30)
Speed 40 ft.

STR	DEX	CON	INT	WIS	CHA
21(+5)	10 (+0)	17 (+3)	3 (−4)	10 (+0)	7 (−2)

Damage Immunities cold
Senses passive Perception 10
Languages —
Challenge 6 (2,300 XP)

Blind Rage. When the snowbeast first takes damage, it becomes enraged, gains 20 temporary hit points, and fights to the death.

Charm Immunity. The snowbeast is immune to all mind-affecting magic such as the *charm monster* spell.

Rend. If the snowbeast hits a single target with both a Bite attack and a Claws attack in the same turn, it inflicts an additional 12 (2d6 + 5) force damage to that target.

Siege Monster. The snowbeast deals double damage to objects and structures.

Actions

Multiattack. The snowbeast makes one Bite attack and one Claws attack.

Bite. Melee Weapon Attack: +8 to hit, reach 5 ft., one target. *Hit:* 10 (1d10 + 5) piercing damage.

Claws. Melee Weapon Attack: +8 to hit, reach 10 ft., one target. *Hit:* 14 (2d8 + 5) slashing damage.

This towering, 12-foot-tall monstrosity with beady yellow eyes is covered in white fur and has a maw of flat, grinding teeth. It wants only to feast and devour, with no greater intellect or plan. It attacks the nearest foe without any thought to tactics or strategy.

The Dentist

Small humanoid (goblinoid), chaotic evil
Armor Class 15 (studded leather armor)
Hit Points 33 (6d6 + 12)
Speed 30 ft.

STR	DEX	CON	INT	WIS	CHA
13(+1)	16 (+3)	14 (+2)	10 (+0)	10 (+0)	10 (+0)

Skills Intimidation +2, Medicine +2, Stealth +5
Senses darkvision 60 ft., passive Perception 10
Languages Common, Goblin

Challenge 1 (200 XP)

Nimble Escape. The Dentist can take the Disengage or Hide action as a bonus action on each of his turns.

Extraction. If The Dentist rolls a 19 or a 20 on a Pliers attack roll and the target creature has teeth, The Dentist has pulled a tooth from his target's mouth.

Actions

Pliers. Melee Weapon Attack: +5 to hit, reach 5 ft., one target. *Hit:* 5 (1d4 + 3) piercing damage. A creature hit by the pliers is grappled by The Dentist (escape DC 14). While grappled, a creature has disadvantage on Dexterity saving throws. If The Dentist starts his turn with a target grappled, he automatically inflicts 10 (2d6 + 3) piercing damage to that target.

Crueltide Contraption (recharge 4-6). The Dentist retrieves one of his deadly contraptions from his bag and begins using it (roll or choose from the table above under Crueltide Elf). The Dentist has +5 on his attack rolls for thrown or fired contraptions. Note: certain contraptions such as Rider Red's Bee-Bee Crossbow may be used for multiple rounds without requiring another use of this ability or successful Recharge roll.

Winter Bones

Large undead, neutral
Armor Class 16 (natural armor)
Hit Points 85 (10d10 + 30)
Speed 40 ft.

STR	DEX	CON	INT	WIS	CHA
14(+2)	19 (+4)	16 (+3)	17 (+3)	13 (+1)	12 (+1)

Saving Throws Dex +7, Int +6, Wis +3
Skills Acrobatics +7, History +9, Nature +9, Perception +3
Damage Resistances lightning, necrotic; piercing and slashing from nonmagical attacks
Damage Immunities cold, poison
Condition Immunities charmed, exhaustion, frightened, paralyzed, poisoned
Senses darkvision 60 ft., passive Perception 13
Languages —
Challenge 6 (2,300 XP)

Turn Resistance. The winter bones has advantage on saving throws against any effect that turns undead.

Actions

Dancing Fool (recharge 6). The winter bones creates a magical compulsion field in a 60-foot radius around itself. Each creature in the area when the effect begins, or who enters the area, must succeed on a DC 15 Wisdom saving throw or dance violently and maniacally, causing harm to itself. An affected creature is restrained and takes 3 (1d6) force damage. The effect lasts for 1 minute, and affected creatures continue to dance even if no longer in the area of effect or if the winter bones is killed. At the start of each of the winter bones' turns, each affected creature takes 3 (1d6) force damage for every round it has been dancing, including the current round. An affected creature may repeat the saving throw at the end of each of its turns, ending the effect on itself on a success. Undead and creatures immune to charm are not affected by this ability. Once a creature succeeds on a saving throw against this effect, it is immune to the winter bones' Dancing Fool ability for 24 hours. Casting *dispel magic* or *remove curse* on an affected creatures removes the effect from that creature.

This strange winter spirits appears to mortal eyes like a frost-ravaged scarecrow that somehow came to life. It is long-limbed and stands more than 7ft tall. It has spindly limbs and a skeletal face and is clad only in a long black tabard. Winter Bones dances merrily through the snow, flitting from tree to tree. Winter Bones moves swiftly and silently through the harsh frozen landscape, never leaving signs of its passing unless it so desires.

If attacked, Winter Bones laughs merrily, dancing deftly around its foes and singing ancient songs of the season.

Winter Bones is not, by nature, a violent creature. He is, however, insanely curious about all things and typically wants only to talk and make inquiries of those he encounters. Only when he is met with violence or extreme rudeness does he use force his enemies to dance for his pleasure and most often he leaves soon after, vanishing into the winter wonderland around him in search of better-behaved playthings. If slain, it is whispered that Winter Bones simply rises again with the next snowfall, as curious as ever.

Appendix B: New Magic Items

Newville Valley is home to several unique magic items that are detailed below.

Frozen Concoction

Potion, uncommon

When you drink this frosty dwarven beverage, you gain a climbing speed equal to your walking speed for 1 hour. During this time, you have advantage on Strength (Athletics) checks you make to climb or to prevent yourself from being disarmed.

Talisman of the Newville Protector

Wondrous item, uncommon (requires attunement)

These simple bronze brooches are shaped like a pockmarked circular shield but have an uncanny resemblance to a chocolate-chip cookie. While attuned and actively defending Newville or its people, you receive a +1 bonus to your Armor Class and to all saving throws. Outside the Newville Valley, these are simple bronze badges.

Cane of Winter's Shepherd

Rod, very rare (requires attunement)

This long white shepherd's crook is striped with a band of red and functions as a *+1 staff* though you gain several additional benefits. First, while you are attuned to the cane, your breath is always minty fresh, and you can cast *purify food and drink* and *neutralize poison* three times per day each. The food or beverage you make is perfectly edible and has a slight mint flavoring.

Dagger of the Winter Wonderland

Weapon (dagger), very rare

This strange poniard resembles a carrot perpetually glazed in frost. It functions as a *+1 dagger* and once per day allows you to reappear on a patch of snow you can see within 100 feet provided you are standing on a patch of snow. In addition, you receive a +2 bonus to all saving throws made against any cold-based effects or damage.

Appendix C:
Orcus' Christmas Slay

How *does* **Orcus' Claws** get around the world in a single night to bring holiday fear to all the little girls and boys on the Prime Material Plane?

Why, with his big red slay — err, sleigh, of course! This massive sleigh is blood red and carved from gnarled, burnt wood. Its runners are rusted with blood and the long bench seat at its front is terribly uncomfortable to sit upon. Its leather reins are burnt black with hellfire and crack with unholy power, while its bells "jingle" with the tiny screams of those who have found themselves on the "naughty list."

If Orcus' Claws is defeated, his *Slay* becomes an unbound magical artifact. The magic laid upon it can be harnessed by adventurers willing to undertake a series of long and difficult quests to gather all the components necessary to operate the Slay. *Orcus' Christmas Slay* is made up of several components: the *sleigh*, the *reins*, and the *bells*. While each of these components has inherent power, when the three are brought together along with Orcus' eight demonic reindeer and bound under a new master, their dark energies are released full upon the world.

The Sleigh

Painted red with blood, set upon rails of the coldest iron, and capable of holding countless corpses in rotting sacks, the *sleigh of Orcus* is a massive wooden sleigh measuring thirty feet long and twenty feet wide. The walls of its bed rise ten feet in the air. It is icy cold to the touch and radiates an unholy aura to any who are sensitive to the presence of the dark powers of the world.

The *sleigh* itself possesses several strange magical properties. It only needs to be pulled by a single horse (who moves at its normal speed when pulling the *sleigh*), though the poor beast of burden withers and sickens after a week of being tasked with pulling the horrid winter sled. In another week, the wretched creature is emaciated to the point of death. This damage is unrecoverable, save by divine intervention or the use of a *wish* spell. If left tied to the *sleigh* overnight, the horse (or other draft beast) rises as a **zombie**, bound forever to the service of the *sleigh* master.

The draft animal, regardless of its form, gains the following features when it reaches the point of becoming undead:

• It becomes an undead, and gains immunity to poison damage and the poisoned condition.

• It gains the following additional features:

Favored Terrain. Whenever the creature is moving through snow covered terrain or blood-soaked battlefields, its speed is doubled.

Undead Fortitude. If damage reduces the creature to 0 hit points, it must make a Constitution saving throw with a DC of 5 + the damage taken, unless the damage is radiant or from a critical hit. On a success, the creature drops to 1 hit point instead.

In addition, the *sleigh* functions as a *portable hole* for any object placed in the bed. The item vanishes in an icy blast of brimstone when placed there and can be recalled by reaching back into the bed at any time. However, each time an item is retrieved there is a cumulative 1% chance that a demonic creature springs forth from this terrible abyssal portal to devour those who would dare deface the *sleigh* of their master.

The *sleigh* itself is impervious to all forms of damage and can only be removed from creation by having a *bless* spell cast upon it, and then *wished* out of existence.

The Reins

The *reins* of *Orcus's Slay* appear at first glance to be a long, leather whip burnt black and laced with shards of jagged metal. In fact, the *reins* function as a *+3 whip* that radiates a faint aura of evil enchantment and functions as a *sword of wounding*.

If the *reins* are brought within fifty feet of Orcus's sleigh, the wielder can use a bonus action to command the *reins* to leap from the hand of their wielder and wrap themselves around the *sleigh*, ready to be held by the driver. While the *sleigh* and the *reins* are together, any character aboard the *sleigh* receives a measure of protection as the *reins* animate to defend them. Anyone within thirty feet of the *sleigh* that is hostile to the *sleigh* or any of its riders finds themselves the target of an animated lashing from the *reins*, which leap out with wicked accuracy on initiative count 20. The *reins* make three attacks with a +6 attack bonus, and inflict 5 (1d4 + 3) slashing damage and inflict wounds as normal.

The *reins*, whether functioning as a whip or as protection for *sleigh* riders, can only be destroyed by having a *bless* spell cast upon then and then *wished* out of existence.

The Bells

The last and most nefarious of Orcus' Christmas Slay are the *bells*. Similar to the *reins*, the *bells* are a string of cold, grey bells cast in lead. Their ring is low and hollow, completely atonal and without any sense of music and beauty. They are set into a broad, three-foot-long black leather strap that matches the *reins*. There is even a tiny clasp on the *bells*, allowing them to be worn as a bracer.

When worn, the *bells* ring with a discordant jangle that all living beings that can hear them find disconcerting and disturbing. Concentration and focus become nigh-impossible as these crackling sounds bounce around inside the skulls of any that hear them. When the wielder makes an attack roll while wearing the *bells* and hits, the target has disadvantage on its next attack roll, and has disadvantage on any Constitution saving throw to maintain concentration until the beginning of its next turn.

If the *bells* are touched to a creature or creatures hitched to the *sleigh*, they wrap around the beast (or beasts) and entwine themselves with the *sleigh*. Such beasts can travel without growing tired from sunset to sunrise and receive a +2 bonus to their Armor Class. However, these poor creatures are forever tainted and must feast on at least one pound of human flesh every day or perish.

Once per day, the wearer can also summon forth a **demonic reindeer**. The demonic reindeer lasts for 1 minute and follows the wearer's commands, though it can only be summoned once per day regardless of how long the creature remains. It is completely loyal to the wearer and if it is destroyed then one week of time must pass before it can be summoned again.

Corruption of Christmas

A character whose alignment is not chaotic evil making use of or carrying one of the artifacts that comprise *Orcus's Christmas Slay* runs the risk of their heart shrinking three times too small. Each time they draw upon the power of any one of the above items, the character must make a DC 17 Charisma saving throw. If the character is carrying two pieces of *Orcus's Christmas Slay*, the DC to resist the taint of *Orcus's Christmas Slay* is 19. If the character has all three components, the DC to resist is 21.

On a failed saving throw, the character's alignment shifts one step towards chaotic evil. On a successful saving throw, the character is immune to the influence of the *Slay* and its components for 24 hours.

Any character who dies while in possession of any one of these artifacts rises from the grave on the following Christmas Eve as a **Crueltide elf**, bound in service to Orcus' Claws. This is an eternal, unbreakable bond. While the character's corpse rots, waiting to return to life as a Crueltide elf, it cannot be resurrected or reincarnated by any power short of a *wish*.

Completing Orcus's Slay

If a character manages to get their hands on all three components and combines the three under the light of winter's full moon, they have summoned forth the heralds of Orcus' Claws — whether they meant to or not.

Eight **demonic reindeer** rise from the snow at compass points around *Orcus's Christmas Slay* and immediately attack the character who brought the components together as well as anyone else within 120 feet that seems to be a threat. They fight with great ferocity, adding a d4 to all attack rolls and saving throws that they make for 1 minute. In addition, they are immune to any and all effects of the various components of *Orcus's Christmas Slay*.

In addition, the *bells* begin to ring endlessly at their arrival, and each creature within 30 feet of the *bells* must make a DC 17 Wisdom saving throws at the beginning of its turns. On a failed saving throw, the target has disadvantage on its next attack roll and on any Constitution saving throws to maintain Concentration. On a successful saving throw, the target is immune to this effect for 24 hours.

If by some miracle the characters are able to defeat the eight demonic reindeer, *Orcus's Christmas Slay* and all its components become forever bound to the character that inflicted the most damage during the battle. That character vanishes on the following midnight, seemingly lost forever. But don't worry, a new Orcus' Claws returns on Christmas Day...

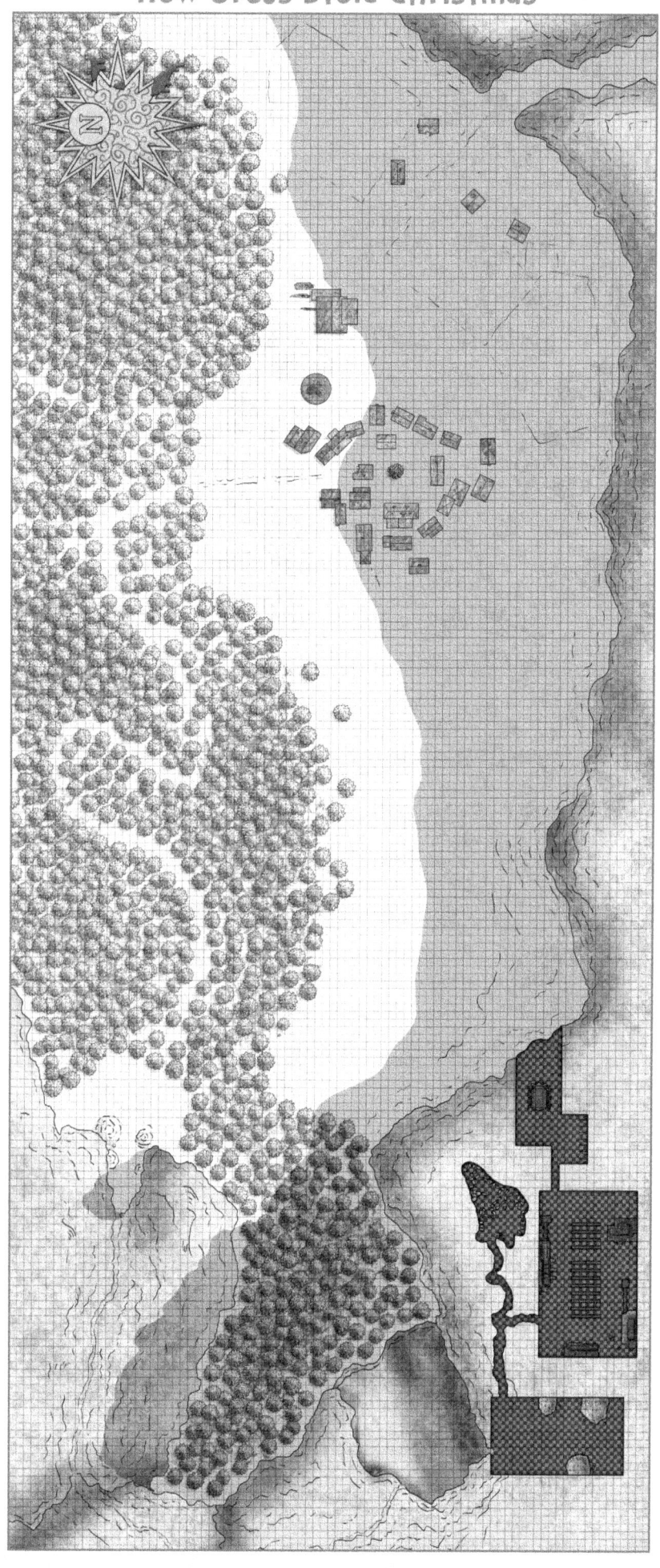